CUBISM
★ IN MY GALLERY ★

WRITTEN BY
EMILIE DUFRESNE

DESIGNED BY
DANIELLE RIPPENGILL

Published in 2022 by Enslow Publishing, LLC
101 W. 23rd Street, Suite 240,
New York, NY 10011

Copyright © 2020 Booklife Publishing
This edition published by arrangement with Booklife Publishing

All rights reserved.

No part of this book may be reproduced by any means without the written permission of the publisher.

Cataloging-in-Publication Data

Names: Dufresne, Emilie.
Title: Cubism / Emilie Dufresne.
Description: New York : Enslow Publishing, 2022. | Series: In my gallery | Includes glossary and index.
Identifiers: ISBN 9781978524071 (pbk.) | ISBN 9781978524095 (library bound) | ISBN 9781978524088 (6 pack) | ISBN 9781978524101 (ebook)
Subjects: LCSH: Cubism--Juvenile literature. | Art, Modern--20th century--Juvenile literature.
Classification: LCC N6494.C8 D843 2022 | DDC 709.04'032--dc2

Designer: Danielle Rippengill
Editor: Madeline Tyler

Printed in the United States of America

CPSIA compliance information: Batch #CS22ENS: For further information contact Enslow Publishing, New York, New York at 1-800-398-2504

IMAGE CREDITS

COVER AND THROUGHOUT – ARTBESOURO, APRIL_PIE, SHTONADO, TASHANATASHA, QUARTA, DANJAZZIA. BACKGROUNDS – EXPRESSVECTORS. CORA & ARTISTS – GRINBOX. GALLERY – GOODSTUDIO, SIBERIAN ART. 2 – HQ VECTORS PREMIUM STUDIO. 5 – ??, 8 – FREEDA. 10 – DELCARMAT, ROMI49. 11 – DMITRIIP, HARE KRISHNA. 14&15 – ELENABSL, KOSMOFISH. 18&19 – HQ VECTORS PREMIUM STUDIO, FOCUS_BELL. 22&23 – VECTORHOT, ALEXANDER RYABINTSEV, MINIWIDE, VECTORPIXELSTAR, BUKHAVETS MIKHAIL. 28&29 – HQ VECTORS PREMIUM STUDIO, VECTORHOT, ALEXANDER RYABINTSEV, MINIWIDE, VECTORPIXELSTAR, BUKHAVETS MIKHAIL. IMAGES ARE COURTESY OF SHUTTERSTOCK.COM. WITH THANKS TO GETTY IMAGES, THINKSTOCK PHOTO AND ISTOCKPHOTO.

CONTENTS

Page 4	Welcome to the Gallery
Page 5	Types of Art
Page 6	Cubism Wing
Page 8	What Is Cubism?
Page 12	Pablo Picasso
Page 14	Activity: Cardboard Instrument
Page 16	Georges Braque
Page 18	Activity: Cubist Still Life
Page 20	Juan Gris
Page 22	Activity: Cubist Collage
Page 24	Alexandra Nechita
Page 26	Activity: Self-Portrait in Shapes
Page 28	Opening Night
Page 30	Quiz
Page 31	Glossary
Page 32	Index

Words that look like **this** are explained in the glossary on page 31.

WELCOME TO THE GALLERY

Hi! I'm Cora and I work in this gallery. It is my job to help find pieces of art in the style of Cubism and put them up in this wing. We are going to learn all about the **movement** of Cubism and make some art! It's time to get started...

Museums and Galleries

Museums and galleries are places that the public can visit to see art. Galleries and museums can either buy or borrow art to show to the public. They also take care of artworks and make sure that they don't get damaged or faded while on display.

TYPES OF ART

You might see lots of different types of art when you visit a gallery or museum. Let's look at some of the types of art that we will see in this book.

Sculpture is when one, or many, materials are put together in a way that creates a 3D object. Picasso created many sculptures during his lifetime.

Painting is when paint is put onto a flat surface, such as a <u>canvas</u>. Paint can be put onto a canvas in many ways, such as brushing, splashing, or scraping. Georges Braque made many Cubist paintings.

Collage is a type of art where different materials are glued onto a flat surface. Juan Gris used to create Cubist collages using different materials.

CUBISM WING

Welcome to the Cubism Wing! The wing is all ready, and now we just need some art. Let's try to make some Cubist pieces.

Some museums and galleries show one type of art or one particular artist's works. This gallery shows lots of different works, from artists across all different movements.

It would be good to get some sculptures on those **plinths** in the middle of the room, and maybe some paintings along this wall and collages over there. This wing is going to be full of Cubism!

CUBISM GOT ITS NAME FROM THE **GEOMETRIC SHAPES** THAT THE ARTISTS USED IN ORDER TO CREATE THEIR ARTWORKS. CUBIST PAINTERS OFTEN MADE THEIR ARTWORKS OUT OF A COLLECTION OF LOTS OF LITTLE CUBES.

Let's learn some more about Cubism so that we can start creating some art!

WHAT IS CUBISM?

Before Cubism

Cubism began in Europe during the early 1900s. Before Cubism, there were many other art movements, two of which were Post-Impressionism and Fauvism. Post-Impressionism began in the late 1800s and Fauvism began at the beginning of the 1900s.

POST-IMPRESSIONISTS LOOKED TO THEIR EMOTIONS AND FEELINGS TO HELP THEM SHOW THE WORLD IN A VERY PERSONAL WAY. FAUVIST ARTISTS MADE EVEN MORE ABSTRACT ART.

POST-IMPRESSIONIST ARTWORK

Fauvist artists made art that didn't show space as the eye sees it. Instead, they would often show things as flat patches of color instead of having depth and shading.

When Art Got Abstract

During the early 1900s, art was becoming more and more abstract. Abstract art doesn't try to show reality in the way we see it in real life. Instead, feelings and emotions are shown through colors and the way the artworks are put together.

FAUVIST ARTWORK

Henri Matisse was a Fauvist artist. He was known for using brightly colored shapes to create simple pictures. One of Matisse's works, *The Snail*, is made of brightly colored squares and rectangles in a spiral pattern – just like a snail's shell. It doesn't look exactly like a snail because it is an abstract piece of art.

All About Angles

Similar to Post-Impressionism and Fauvism, Cubism changed how objects were shown in space. Instead of showing them as the eye sees them, Cubist artists would try to show an object from lots of different **perspectives**.

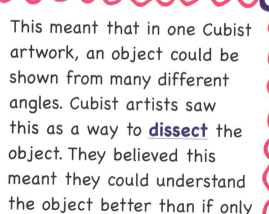

CUBIST ARTWORK

CUBIST ARTWORK

This meant that in one Cubist artwork, an object could be shown from many different angles. Cubist artists saw this as a way to **dissect** the object. They believed this meant they could understand the object better than if only one perspective was shown.

Types of Cubism

Cubism can be split into two main types: Analytical Cubism and Synthetic Cubism. The earlier part of the movement was known as Analytical Cubism. Analytical Cubism used **natural** and dark colors and the artworks were often more **fragmented**.

Synthetic Cubism came after Analytical Cubism. This type of Cubism tended to show simpler images with simpler shapes and perspectives. Synthetic Cubists began experimenting with collage and newspaper in their works, as well as making images flatter and less 3D.

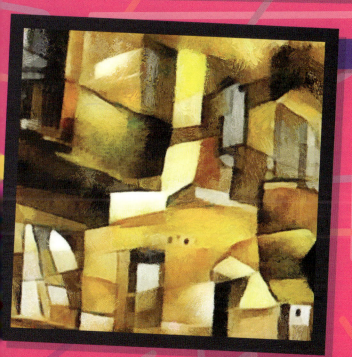

SYNTHETIC CUBISM

ANALYTICAL CUBISM

PABLO PICASSO

Country of Birth: Spain
Born: 1881
Died: 1973 (aged 91)

Pablo Picasso was one of the pioneers of Cubism. Before Picasso began creating Cubist work, he worked in many other styles. For example, during his Rose Period and Blue Period, he focused on certain color palettes, such as pinks and blues.

Picasso pushed abstract art to new and exciting places. Picasso created Cubist paintings, sculptures, and ceramics. Later in the Cubist movement, Picasso began adding newspapers and wrappers to his collages. This made people question what was real in the collage and what wasn't. Picasso created a cardboard sculpture of a guitar. This sculpture was revolutionary because sculptures were usually made out of metal or wood, not cardboard.

Picasso wasn't afraid to experiment and try new ways of making art that hadn't been done before. Picasso's art went on to influence later abstract art movements.

Activity:
CARDBOARD INSTRUMENT

You will need:

- A cardboard box ☑
- Scissors ☑
- A pencil ☑
- Masking tape ☑
- String ☑

Let's try to create a Cubist sculpture like Picasso. I'm going to make a guitar, but you can choose any instrument you want, such as a violin, flute, or drum.

First, try to think about dissecting the instrument into shapes. I am going to use a long, thin rectangle for the neck of the guitar, some circles for the tuning pegs, a figure-eight shape for the bottom, and some circles for the hole in the middle.

Flatten out the cardboard box. Using a pencil, draw the shapes you are going to need on the cardboard and cut them out.

Remember to cut out shapes that you can see from all different angles of the instrument. This will mean that from the front of your sculpture you might also be able to see the side.

Lay out your pieces of cardboard until you are happy.

Use the tape to attach all of your pieces. You can add strings to your instrument too.

GEORGES BRAQUE

Country of Birth: France
Born: 1882
Died: 1963 (aged 81)

Georges Braque was another pioneer of Cubism. Throughout his life, he mainly focused on painting, but in later years he created collages and sculptures as well.

Braque began as a Fauvist artist but began to create Cubist artworks after meeting Picasso. The artworks that he created throughout his life were often **still lifes**, and this didn't change when he began creating Cubist artworks.

Braque was very interested in how space and perspectives are shown. His paintings of Cubist still lifes were very detailed and showed so many perspectives that they looked like complex patterns. During the Synthetic Cubist period, Braque also made Cubist collages and was known to add materials such as wallpaper and sawdust to his paintings.

Activity:
CUBIST STILL LIFE

You will need:

- A camera
- A fruit bowl
- Various pieces of fruit
- A printer
- Scissors
- Glue
- Thick paper or cardboard

Let's try to make a Cubist still life using photographs!

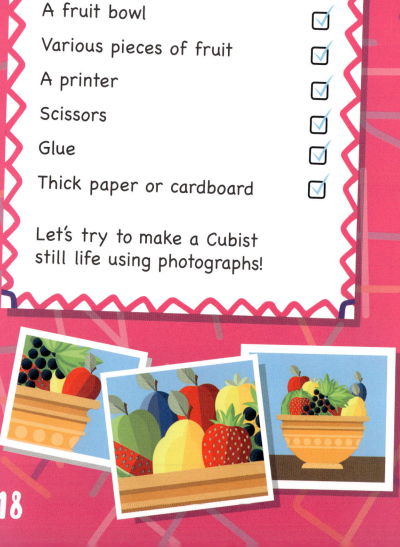

Place the fruit in the fruit bowl.

Put the fruit bowl on a table or on the floor and make sure there is nothing near it.

Now use the camera to take lots of photos of the fruit bowl from different perspectives, all around the fruit bowl.

Print the photos. Cut out the bowl and each piece of fruit from every photo. Put the different cutouts into piles so that you know which pile is of which fruit.

Arrange the pieces on the paper.

Try to keep the same fruit in the same area. Don't be afraid to layer lots of different pieces and perspectives on top of each other.

When you are happy with how everything looks, glue it down.

JUAN GRIS

Country of Birth: Spain
Born: 1887
Died: 1927 (aged 40)

Juan Gris was friends with both Picasso and Braque when he lived in Paris. Gris began creating Cubist artworks around 1910. He soon started creating Synthetic Cubist works. His style of Synthetic Cubism was different from that of Picasso and Braque.

He would not break up an image as much as other Cubist artists. Instead, he would cut strips or fragments out of newspapers and advertisements. In his still-life collages, he would show the view from above the still life and fragment the image with sharp-edged pieces to help him create a simpler Cubist style than Picasso and Braque. He also tried to show the textures of different materials such as cloth and wood in his collages.

It is thought Gris's use of these objects in his collages went on to inspire artworks of the Dada and Pop Art movements.

Activity:
CUBIST COLLAGE

You will need:

- Cereal boxes ✓
- Newspaper ✓
- Breakfast table ✓
- Scissors ✓
- Glue ✓
- Two sheets of thick paper or cardboard ✓
- A pencil
- An eraser ✓
- Colored pencils ✓
- Paint ✓
- A ruler ✓

Let's make a collage of our breakfast table, just like Gris.

Set your table for breakfast. Make sure you have some of the food you usually eat on the table, such as cereal and bread.

Sketch out how the table looks. Don't worry, it doesn't need to look like a Cubist painting yet! Once your sketch is finished, take your ruler and draw four lines through your sketch. Now cut along the lines so that your sketch is in different strips.

On another piece of paper, draw an empty table. Don't forget to try drawing the texture of the table. Cut out parts of the newspaper and cereal boxes. Stick them, and your cut-up drawing, over your drawing of the empty table. If you want to, use the colored pencils and paint to make it colorful.

ALEXANDRA NECHITA

Country of Birth: Romania
Born: 1985

Alexandra Nechita is a <u>contemporary</u> artist who began painting at a very young age. She quickly became very successful and held her first art exhibition at the age of eight. Her works have been shown in exhibitions across the world, and she is still creating art today in the U.S.

Her work is often compared to that of the Cubists of the early 1900s because she breaks things up into geometric shapes. However, she also uses very bright and <u>vibrant</u> colors, which people see as very <u>expressive</u>. Even at a young age, she experimented with different types of art including pen and ink, watercolors, oil paintings, and sculpture. Her paintings often show people with body parts made of strange shapes that are too long or the wrong size.

Activity:
SELF-PORTRAIT IN SHAPES

You will need:

Thick paper or cardboard ☑

A pencil ☑

Paints in lots of colors ☑

Paintbrushes ☑

We are going to try to make a self-portrait in the style of Nechita. Let's see what we can do!

First, it's time to sketch your self-portrait. Remember, Nechita often makes things the wrong shape or size.

I have chosen a heart shape for my lips, and a big circle for the bottom of my hair. I have also made my eye a lot bigger than it looks in real life. Lastly, I have shown my neck as a rectangle. What shapes will you use to show your body parts?

Once you have finished your sketch, get your paints ready.

Paint different parts of your body in different colors. I have chosen blues and greens because they are my favorite colors, but you can choose any colors you want.

Be as bold and as bright as you want to be!

OPENING NIGHT

The wing is open! Look at all the amazing artworks we have created. They look great. I wonder what everyone is talking about...

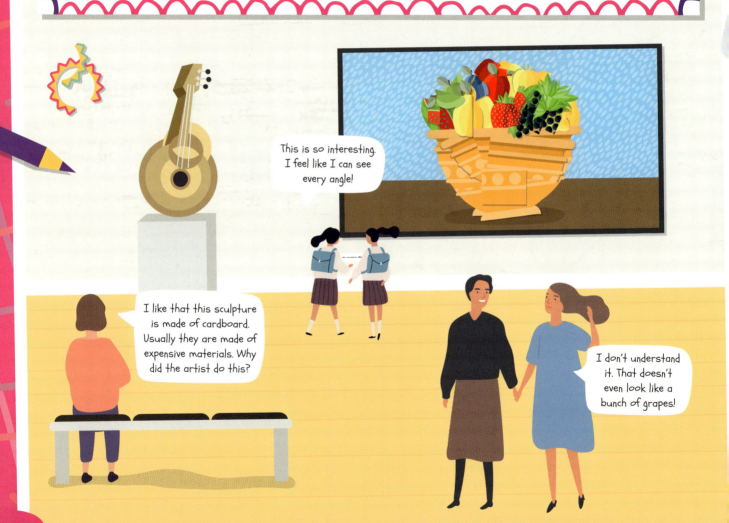

It is important to talk about how art makes us feel. There are no right or wrong answers when talking about art. Art can make us feel and think different things. How do you feel about your art? What do you like about it?

QUIZ

1. Can you name two art movements that came before Cubism?
2. Which artist created *The Snail*?
3. What type of art did Georges Braque often create?
4. What country was Juan Gris born in?
5. Which artist held their first exhibition at the age of eight?

Answers: 1. Post-Impressionism and Fauvism 2. Henri Matisse 3. Still lifes 4. Spain 5. Alexandra Nechita

Have you ever visited a gallery or museum?

Why not see if there is one near you that you could visit? It might inspire you to create more art, or to talk about how the art makes you feel. If you see any artworks that you like, why not try to create a piece of art in the same style at home?

GLOSSARY

canvas	a woven fabric that is pulled tightly over a frame to create a blank space to be painted on
ceramics	pieces of art that are made of baked clay
color palettes	groups of colors that an artist might use for one painting or for a period of time
contemporary	belonging to the current time period
Dada	a type of art that was nonsensical and unlike any type of art that had come before it
depth and shading	a technique used to make objects in paintings look more realistic and 3D
dissect	to take apart and look at, or think about, carefully
expressive	showing feelings and emotions
Fauvism	an art movement that was very expressive and used unnatural colors
fragmented	broken into pieces
geometric shapes	shapes such as triangles, squares, and circles
inspire	to influence to do something
movement	a category or type of art that an artwork or artist might belong to, which can sometimes be related to a certain time or place
natural	found in the world and produced by nature
perspectives	viewpoints or ways of looking at something
pioneers	people who are the first to do something new or in a new way
plinths	bases or columns that support statues, sculptures, or artworks
Pop Art	an art movement that was heavily influenced by things in popular culture such as celebrities, advertisements, and comics
Post-Impressionism	an art movement that moved away from Impressionism and showed how memory and emotion influence how people see the world
revolutionary	doing something in a way that drastically changes how it is done or thought of
sketch	to do a quick drawing, often in pencil
still lifes	paintings or drawings of objects that aren't living, such as fruit, bottles, bowls, and glasses
vibrant	bright and colorful

31

INDEX

A
abstract 8, 9, 12

C
collage 5, 7, 11–12, 16, 20, 22–23
Cubism
- Analytical 11
- Synthetic 11, 16, 20

D
Dada 20

E
expression 24

F
Fauvism 8–10, 16
fruit 18–19

M
Matisse, Henri 9

P
painting 5, 7, 12, 16, 22–24, 26–27
photography 18–19
Pop Art 20
Post-Impressionism 8, 10

S
sculpture 5–7, 12, 14–16, 24, 28
self-portraits 26–27
shapes 7, 9, 11, 15, 24, 27
sketching 23, 27
still lifes 16, 18, 20